Adapted from the translation
by
Mrs. H.B. Paull

Illustrations Copyright © 1982 by Katie Thamer
First Edition • First Printing
ISBN 0-914676-82-2
Green Tiger Press
La Jolla
92038

HANS ANDERSEN

THE
RED
SHOES

Illustrations by

KATIE THAMER

A STAR & ELEPHANT BOOK

1982

There was once a little girl who was very pretty and delicate; but in summer she used to go barefooted, because she was poor. In winter she wore large wooden shoes, and her little feet became sore and red.

In the village lived an old shoemaker's wife, who had some old strips of red cloth; and these she sewed together, as well as she could, into a little pair of shoes. They were rather clumsy, but they were made with kind intentions, for they were to be given to the little girl, whose name was Karen.

The shoes were given to her, and she wore them for the first time on the day her mother was buried. They were certainly not suitable for mourning, but she had no others, so she put them on her bare feet, and walked behind the poor pine coffin.

A large old-fashioned carriage passed by, in which sat an old lady. She looked at the little girl, and felt pity for her, so she said to the clergyman, "Pray give me that little girl, and I will care for her."

Karen believed that it was all because of the red shoes that this good fortune had befallen her. The old lady, however, thought the shoes hideous, and had them burnt. Karen herself was dressed in neat and tidy clothes, and was taught to read and to sew. And people said that she was pretty, but her mirror said, "You are more than pretty; you are beautiful."

Not long after, a queen traveled through the country with her little daughter, who was a princess, and crowds flocked to the castle to see them. Karen was amongst them, and she saw the little princess in a white dress, standing at a window, to allow everyone to gaze upon her. She had neither train nor golden crown on her head, but she wore a beautiful pair of red morocco shoes, much better than those that the old shoemaker's wife had made for little Karen. Surely nothing in the world could be compared with those red shoes.

The time arrived for Karen to be Confirmed. New clothes were made for her, and she was to have, also, a pair of new shoes. A rich shoemaker in the town took the measure of her little foot at his own house, in a room where stood large glass cases full of elegant shoes and shining boots. They looked beautiful, but the old lady could not see very well, so she did not take much pleasure in looking at them. Among the shoes stood a pair of red ones, just like those which the princess had worn. Oh, how pretty they were! The shoemaker said they had been made for a count's daughter, but they had not fitted her properly.

"Are they of polished leather?" said the old lady. "They shine as if they were."

"Yes, they do shine," said Karen, and she tried them on. They fit her and were bought, but the old lady did not know they were red. She would never have allowed Karen to go to Confirmation in red shoes.

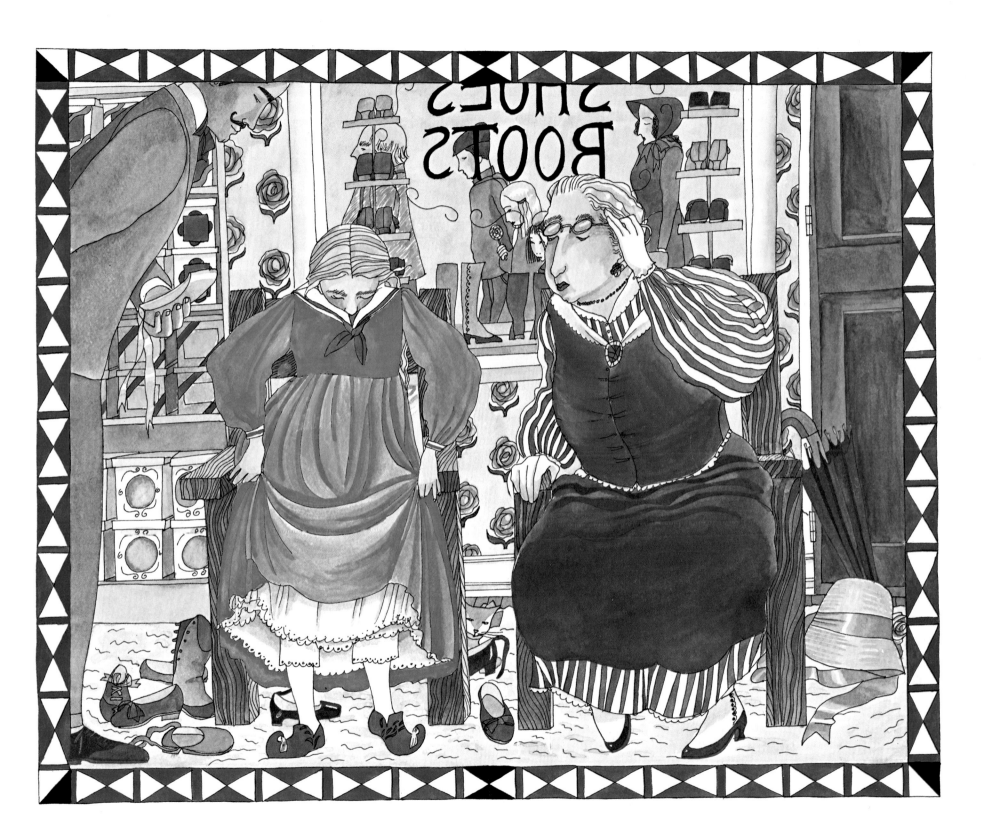

Everyone looked at her feet, and as she passed through the church, to the entrance of the choir, it seemed as if the old pictures on the tombs, and the portraits of clergymen and their wives, with their stiff collars and long black dresses, were all fixing their eyes on her red shoes. She thought only of her shoes, even when the clergyman laid his hands on her head, and spoke of her Baptism, and of her covenant with God, and that now she must remember to act as a grown-up Christian. The organ pealed forth its solemn tones, and the fresh, young voices of the children sounded sweetly as they joined with the choir, but Karen thought only of her red shoes.

In the afternoon the old lady was told by everyone that the shoes were red. She said it was very shocking, and not at all proper, and she told Karen that when she went to church in the future, she must always wear black shoes, even though they might be old.

The following Sunday was Sacrament Sunday, and Karen was to receive Holy Communion for the first time. She looked first at her black shoes, and then at the red ones; then she looked at the red again—and she put them on.

The sun shone brightly, and Karen and the old lady went to church by the footpath through the fields, for the road was so dusty.

Near the church door stood an old soldier, with a crutch and a wonderfully long beard, more red than white. He bowed nearly to the ground, and asked the old lady if he might wipe her shoes. And Karen stretched out her foot also.

"Ah, what pretty dancing shoes," exclaimed the soldier. "Mind you stick fast when she dances." As he spoke he struck the soles of her shoes with his hand.

Everyone in the church looked at Karen's red shoes, and the figures in the portraits gazed too. When she knelt at the altar, and took the golden chalice to her lips, she thought only of her red shoes, and it seemed that they floated before her eyes in the depths of the cup. She did not take part in singing the hymn of praise, and she forgot to say the Lord's Prayer. Then all the people went out of church, and the old lady stepped into her carriage. Karen lifted her foot to step in also, and the old soldier cried, "See what beautiful dancing shoes."

And then Karen found she could not help dancing a few steps, and when she began, it seemed as if her legs would go on dancing. It was just as if the shoes had a power over her. She danced round the corner of the church, and could not stop herself. The coachman was obliged to run after her and catch her, and lift her into the carriage. But even then her feet went on dancing, so that she kept treading on the good old lady's toes. At last she took off the shoes, and then her legs were able to rest. As soon as they reached home, the shoes were put away in a closet; but Karen could not resist looking at them.

Soon after this the old lady was taken ill, and it was said that she could not recover. She had to be waited upon and nursed, and no one ought to have been so anxious to do this as Karen. There was to be a grand ball in the town, however, to which Karen was invited. She thought of the old lady, who after all could not recover. She looked at the red shoes—there was no harm in looking. She told herself that there could be no wrong in putting them on; nor was there. But then she went to the ball, and began to dance.

However, the shoes would not let her do as she wished. When she wanted to go to the right, they would dance to the left; or if she wished to go up the floor, they persisted in going down. At last they danced down the stairs, into the street, and out of the town gate. She danced on in spite of herself, till she came to a gloomy wood. Something was shining up among the trees. At first she thought it was the moon, and then she saw a face. It was the old soldier, with his red beard; and he sat and nodded to her, and said, "See what pretty dancing shoes they are."

At that, she grew frightened, and she tried to pull off the red shoes, but they clung fast. She tore off her stockings, but still the shoes remained; they seemed to have grown to her feet. And she danced, as dance she must—over fields and meadows, in rain and in sunshine, by night and by day. It was most terrible at night.

She danced through the lonely churchyard. The dead there do not dance; they are better employed. She would gladly have rested, even on a poor man's grave, where bitter tansy grew, but for her there was neither rest nor peace. She danced towards the open church door. There before it was an angel, in long white robes, with wings that reached from his shoulders down to the ground. His countenance was grave and stern, and in his hand he held a bright and flaming sword.

"Dance you shall," said he. "Dance in your red shoes till you are pale and cold, till your skin shrivels up and you are a skeleton! Dance you shall, from door to door, and where proud, haughty children live you shall knock, so they may hear you and be afraid! Dance you shall!"

"Mercy!" cried Karen, but she did not hear what the angel answered, for her shoes carried her away from the door, into the fields and over the paths and byways; dancing, ever dancing.

One morning she danced by a door which she knew well. She could hear sounds of singing within, and a coffin decked with flowers was presently carried out. Then Karen knew that the old lady was dead, and she felt at that moment that she had been forsaken by all the world, as well as condemned by an angel of God.

Still must she dance through the long days, and the dark, gloomy nights. The shoes carried her on through brambles, and over stumps of trees, which scratched her till the blood came. Finally she danced across a heath to a little lonely house. Here, she knew, the executioner dwelt. She tapped with her fingers on the window-pane, and said, "Come out, come out; I cannot come in, for I must dance."

And the executioner said, "Do you not know who I am? I am he who cuts off the heads of the wicked; already my axe tingles to do so."

"Do not strike off my head," said Karen, "for then I shall not be able to repent of my sin; but cut off my feet with the red shoes." So she confessed all her sins, and the executioner cut off her feet with the red shoes on them, and the shoes with the little feet in them danced away over the fields and were lost in the dark wood. And he cut out a pair of wooden feet for her, and gave her crutches. Then he taught her a psalm, which the penitents always sing, and she kissed the hand that had wielded the axe, and went away across the heath.

"Now I have suffered enough for the red shoes," said she, "I will go to church, that I may be seen there by the people." And she went as quickly as she could to the church door, but when she arrived, the red shoes were there, and they danced before her eyes, and frightened her so that she turned back.

Through the whole week she was in anguish, and wept many bitter tears; but when Sunday came again, she said, "Now I have suffered and striven enough; I believe I am quite as good as many of those who sit holding their heads so high in church." She went boldly forth, but she did not get further than the churchyard gate, for there were the red shoes dancing before her. Now she was truly afraid, and went back, and repented of her sinful pride with her whole heart.

She went to the parsonage and begged to be taken in there as a servant, promising to be industrious, and do all that she could, even without wages. All she craved was the shelter of a home, and the company of good people. The clergyman's wife had pity on Karen, and took her into her service. Karen proved industrious and thoughtful. Silently she sat and listened when the clergyman read the Bible aloud in the evening. All the little ones loved her, but when they chattered about dress, or finery, or about being as beautiful as a queen, she would sadly shake her head.

On Sunday they all went to church, and they asked her if she would like to go with them; but she looked sorrowfully and with tearful eyes at her crutches. While the others went to listen to God's word, she sat alone in her little room, which was only just large enough to contain a bed and a chair. Here she remained with her hymn-book in her hand, and as she read in a humble spirit, the wind wafted the tones of the organ from the church towards her, and she lifted her tearful face, and said, "O Lord, help me."

Suddenly the sun shone brightly, and before her stood the angel in long white robes, the same whom she had seen on that night at the church door. He no longer held in his hand a sharp sword, but a beautiful green branch covered with roses, and as he touched the ceiling with it, the ceiling became lofty, and bright golden stars sparkled where the branch had touched. The angel touched the walls, and they opened wide, so that she could see the organ whose tones sounded so melodious. She saw, too, the pictures of the clergymen and their wives, and the congregation sitting on the ornamental seats, and singing out of their hymn-books. The church itself had come to the poor girl in her narrow room, or perhaps the room had become a church to her. She found herself sitting on a seat with the rest of the clergyman's servants, and when they had finished the psalm, they looked at her and nodded, and said, "It was right of you to come, Karen."

"It was through God's mercy that I came," said she. The organ pealed forth again, and the children's voices sounded soft and sweet. The bright sunshine streamed through the window, and fell clear and warm upon the chair on which Karen sat. Her heart became so filled with sunshine, peace, and joy, that it broke, and her soul flew on a sunbeam to heaven, where no one asked about the red shoes.

The text was set in Zapf International Medium
by Central Graphics of San Diego.
Book & cover design
by Sandra Darling & Judythe Sieck.
Color separations
by Photolitho, AG., Zurich, Switzerland.
Printed at The Green Tiger Press
in the spring of 1982.